The Spirit Of Christmas

By

Henry Van Dyke

The Spirit of Christmas

A DREAMSTORY

THE CHRISTMAS ANGEL

It was the hour of rest in the Country Beyond the Stars. All the silver bells that swing with the turning of the great ring of light which lies around that land were softly chiming; and the sound of their commotion went down like dew upon the golden ways of the city, and the long alleys of blossoming trees, and the meadows of asphodel, and the curving shores of the River of Life.

At the hearing of that chime, all the angels who had been working turned to play, and all who had been playing gave themselves joyfully to work. Those who had been singing, and making melody on different instruments, fell silent and began to listen. Those who had been walking alone in meditation met together in companies to talk. And those who had been far away on errands to the Earth and other planets came homeward like a flight of swallows to the high cliff when the day is over.

It was not that they needed to be restored from weariness, for the inhabitants of that country never say, "I am tired." But there, as here, the law of change is the secret of happiness, and the joy that never ends is woven of mingled strands of labour and repose, society and solitude, music and silence. Sleep comes to them not as it does to us, with a darkening of the vision and a folding of the wings of the spirit, but with an opening   of the eyes to deeper and fuller light, and with an effortless outgoing of the soul upon broader currents of life, as the sunloving bird poises and circles upward, without a wingbeat, on the upholding air.

It was in one of the quiet corners of the green valley called Peacefield, where the little brook of Brighthopes runs smoothly down to join the River of Life, that I saw a company of angels, returned from various labours on Earth, sitting in friendly converse on the hillside, where cyclamens and arbutus and violets and fringed orchids and pale lady'stresses, and all the sweetsmelling flowers which are separated in the lower world by the seasons, were thrown together in a harmony of fragrance. There were three of the company who seemed to   be leaders, distinguished not only by more radiant and powerful looks, but by a tone of authority in their speech and by the willing attention with which the others listened to them, as they talked of their earthly tasks, of the tangles and troubles, the wars and miseries that they had seen among men, and of the best way to get rid of them and bring sorrow to an end.

"The Earth is full of oppression and unrighteousness," said the tallest and most powerful of the angels. His voice was deep and strong, and by his shining armour and the long twohanded sword hanging over his shoulder I knew that he was the archangel Michael, the mightiest one among the warriors of the King, and the executor of the divine judgments upon the unjust. "The Earth is tormented   with injustice," he cried, "and the great misery that I have seen among men is that the evil hand is often stronger than the good hand and can beat it down.

"The arm of the cruel is heavier than the arm of the kind. The unjust get the better of the just and tread on them. I have seen tyrant kings crush their helpless folk. I have seen the fields of the innocent trampled into bloody ruin by the feet of conquering armies. I have seen the wicked nation overcome the peoples that loved liberty, and take away their treasure by force of arms. I have seen poverty mocked by arrogant wealth, and purity deflowered by brute violence, and gentleness and fairdealing bruised in the winepress of iniquity and pride.

"There is no cure for this evil, but by the giving of greater force to the good hand. The righteous cause must be strengthened with might to resist the wicked, to defend the helpless, to punish all cruelty and unfairness, to uphold the right everywhere, and to enforce justice with unconquerable arms. Oh, that the host of Heaven might be called, arrayed, and sent to mingle in the wars of men, to make the good victorious, to destroy all evil, and to make the will of the King prevail!

"We would shake down the thrones of tyrants, and loose the bands of the oppressed. We would hold the cruel and violent with the bit of fear, and drive the greedy and fierceminded men with the whip of terror. We would stand guard, with weapons drawn, about the innocent, the gentle, the kind, and keep the peace of God with the sword of the angels!"

As he spoke, his hands were lifted to the hilt of his long blade, and he raised it above him, straight and shining, throwing sparkles of light around it, like the spray from the sharp prow of a moving ship. Bright flames of heavenly ardour leaped in the eyes of the listening angels; a martial air passed over their faces as if they longed for the call to war.

But no silver trumpet blared from the battlements of the City of God; no crimson flag was unfurled on those high, secret walls; no thrilling drumbeat echoed over the smooth meadow. Only the sound of the brook of Brighthopes was heard tinkling   and murmuring among the roots of the grasses and flowers; and far off a cadence of song drifted down from the inner courts of the Palace of the King.

Then another angel began to speak, and made answer to Michael. He, too, was tall and wore the look of power. But it was power of the mind rather than of the hand. His face was clear and glistening, and his eyes were lit with a steady flame which neither leaped nor fell. Of flame also were his garments, which clung about him as the fire enwraps a torch burning where there is no wind; and his great wings, spiring to a point far above his head, were like a living lamp before the altar of the Most High. By this sign I knew that it was the archangel Uriel, the spirit of the Sun,   clearest in vision, deepest in wisdom of all the spirits that surround the throne.

"I hold not the same thought," said he, "as the great archangel Michael; nor, though I desire the same end which he desires, would I seek it by the same way. For I know how often power has been given to the good, and how often it has been turned aside and used for evil. I know that the host of Heaven, and the very stars in their courses, have fought on the side of a favoured nation; yet pride has followed triumph and oppression has been the firstborn child of victory. I know that the deliverers of the people have become tyrants over those whom they have set free, and the fighters for liberty have been changed into the soldiers of fortune.   Power corrupts itself, and might cannot save.

"Does not the Prince Michael remember how the angel of the Lord led the armies of Israel, and gave them the battle against every foe, except the enemy within the camp? And how they robbed and crushed the peoples against whom they had fought for freedom? And how the wickedness of the tribes of Canaan survived their conquest and overcame their conquerors, so that the children of Israel learned to worship the idols of their enemies, Moloch, and Baal, and Ashtoreth?

"Power corrupts itself, and might cannot save. Was not Persia the destroyer of Babylon, and did not the tyranny of Persia cry aloud for destruction? Did not Rome break the yoke of the East, and does not the yoke of Rome lie heavy on the shoulders of the world? Listen!"

There was silence for a moment on the slopes of Peacefield, and then over the encircling hills a cool wind brought the sound of chains clanking in prisons and galleys, the sighing of millions of slaves, the weeping of wretched women and children, the blows of hammers nailing men to their crosses. Then the sound passed by with the wind, and Uriel spoke again:

"Power corrupts itself, and might cannot save. The Earth is full of ignorant strife, and for this evil there is no cure but by the giving of greater knowledge. It is because men do not understand evil that they yield themselves to its power. Wickedness   is folly in action, and injustice is the error of the blind. It is because men are ignorant that they destroy one another, and at last themselves.

"If there were more light in the world there would be no sorrow. If the great King who knows all things would enlighten the world with wisdomwisdom to understand his law and his ways, to read the secrets of the earth and the stars, to discern the workings of the heart of man and the things that make for joy and peaceif he would but send us, his messengers, as a flame of fire to shine upon those who sit in darkness, how gladly would we go to bring in the new day!

"We would speak the word of warning and counsel to the erring, and tell knowledge to the perplexed.   We would guide the ignorant in the paths of prudence, and the young would sit at our feet and hear us gladly in the school of life. Then folly would fade away as the morning vapour, and the sun of wisdom would shine on all men, and the peace of God would come with the counsel of the angels."

A murmur of pleasure followed the words of Uriel, and eager looks flashed around the circle of the messengers of light as they heard the praise of wisdom fitly spoken. But there was one among them on whose face a shadow of doubt rested, and though he smiled, it was as if he remembered something that the others had forgotten. He turned to an angel near him.

"Who was it," said he, "to whom   you were sent with counsel long ago? Was it not Balaam the son of Beor, as he was riding to meet the King of Moab? And did not even the dumb beast profit more by your instruction than the man who rode him? And who was it," he continued, turning to Uriel, "that was called the wisest of all men, having searched out and understood the many inventions that are found under the sun? Was not Solomon, prince of fools and philosophers, unable by much learning to escape weariness of the flesh and despair of the spirit? Knowledge also is vanity and vexation. This I know well, because I have dwelt among men and held converse with them since the day when I was sent to instruct the first man in Eden."

Then I looked more closely at him   who was speaking and recognised the beauty of the archangel Raphael, as it was pictured long ago:

"A seraph winged; six wings he wore to shade
His lineaments divine; the pair that clad
Each shoulder broad came mantling o'er his breast,
With regal ornament; the middle pair
Girt like a starry zone his waist, and round
Skirted his loins and thighs with downy gold
And colours dipped in Heav'n; the third his feet
Shadowed from either heel with feathered mail,

Skytinctured grain. Like Maia's son he stood
And shook his plumes, that Heavenly fragrance filled
The circuit wide."

"Too well I know," he spoke on, while the smile on his face deepened into a look of pity and tenderness and desire, "too well I know that power corrupts itself and that knowledge cannot save. There is no cure for the evil that is in the world but by the giving of more love to men. The laws that are ordained for earth are strange and unequal, and the ways where men must walk are full of pitfalls and dangers. Pestilence creeps along the ground and flows in the rivers; whirlwind and tempest shake the habitations of men and drive their ships to destruction; fire breaks forth from the mountains and the foundations of the world tremble. Frail is the flesh of man, and many are his pains and troubles. His children can never find peace until they learn to love one another and to help one another.

"Wickedness is begotten by disease and misery. Violence comes from poverty and hunger. The cruelty of oppression is when the strong tread the weak under their feet; the bitterness of pride is when the wise and learned despise the simple; the crown of folly is when the rich think they are gods, and the poor think that God is not.

"Hatred and envy and contempt are the curse of life. And for these there is no remedy save lovethe will to give and to blessthe will of the King himself, who gives to all and is loving unto every man. But how shall the hearts of men be won to this will? How shall it enter into them and possess them? Even the gods that men fashion for themselves are cruel and proud and false and unjust. How shall the miracle be wrought in human nature to reveal the meaning of humanity? How shall men be made like God?"

At this question a deep hush fell around the circle, and every listener was still, even as the rustling leaves hang motionless when the light breeze falls away in the hour of sunset. Then through the silence, like the song of a faraway thrush from its hermitage in the forest, a voice came ringing: "I know it, I know it, I know it."

Clear and sweetclear as a ray of light, sweeter than the smallest silver bell that rang the hour of restwas that slender voice floating on the odorous and translucent air. Nearer and nearer it came, echoing down the valley, "I know it, I know it, I know it!"

Then from between the rounded hills, among which the brook of Brighthopes is born, appeared a young angel, a little child, with flying hair of gold, and green wreaths twined about his shoulders, and fluttering hands that played upon the air and seemed to lift him so lightly that he had no need of wings. As thistledown, blown by the wind, dances across the water, so he came along the little stream, singing clear above the murmur of the brook.

All the angels rose and turned to look at him with wondering eyes. Multitudes of others came flying swiftly to the place from which the strange, new song was sounding. Rank within rank, like a garden of living flowers, they stood along the sloping banks of the brook while the childangel floated into the midst of them, singing:

"I know it, I know it, I know it! Man shall be made like God because the Son of God shall become a man."

At this all the angels looked at one another with amazement, and gathered more closely about the childangel, as those who hear wonderful news.

"How can this be?" they asked. "How is it possible that the Son of God should be a man?"

"I do not know," said the young angel. "I only know that it is to be."

"But if he becomes a man," said Raphael, "he will be at the mercy of men; the cruel and the wicked will have power upon him; he will suffer."

"I know it," answered the young angel, "and by suffering he will understand the meaning of all sorrow and pain; and he will be able to comfort every one who cries; and his own tears will be for the healing of sad hearts; and those who are healed by him will learn for his sake to be kind to each other."

"But if the Son of God is a true man," said Uriel, "he must first be a child, simple, and lowly, and helpless. It may be that he will never gain the learning of the schools. The masters of earthly wisdom will despise him and speak scorn of him."

"I know it," said the young angel, "but in meekness will he answer them; and to those who become as little children he will give the heavenly wisdom that comes, without seeking, to the pure and gentle of heart."

"But if he becomes a man," said Michael, "evil men will hate and persecute him: they may even take his life, if they are stronger than he."

"I know it," answered the young angel, "they will nail him to a cross. But when he is lifted up, he will draw all men unto him, for he will still be the Son of God, and no heart that is open to love can help loving him, since his love for men is so great that he is willing to die for them."

"But how do you know these things?" cried the other angels. "Who are you?"

"I am the Christmas angel," he said. "At first I was sent as the dream of a little child, a holy child, blessed and wonderful, to dwell in the heart of a pure virgin, Mary of Nazareth. There I was hidden till the word came to call me back to the throne   of the King, and tell me my name, and give me my new message. For this is Christmas day on Earth, and today the Son of God is born of a woman. So I must fly quickly, before the sun rises, to bring the good news to those happy men who have been chosen to receive them."

As he said this, the young angel rose, with arms outspread, from the green meadow of Peacefield and, passing over the bounds of Heaven, dropped swiftly as a shootingstar toward the night shadow of the Earth. The other angels followed hima throng of dazzling forms, beautiful as a rain of jewels falling from the darkblue sky. But the childangel went more swiftly than the others, because of the certainty of gladness in his heart.

And as the others followed him they wondered who had been favoured and chosen to receive the glad tidings.

"It must be the Emperor of the World and his counsellors," they thought. But the flight passed over Rome.

"It may be the philosophers and the masters of learning," they thought. But the flight passed over Athens.

"Can it be the High Priest of the Jews, and the elders and the scribes?" they thought. But the flight passed over Jerusalem.

It floated out over the hill country of Bethlehem; the throng of silent angels holding close together, as if perplexed and doubtful; the childangel darting on far in advance, as one who knew the way through the darkness.

The villages were all still: the very houses seemed asleep; but in one place there was a low sound of talking in a stable, near to an inna sound as of a mother soothing her baby to rest.

All over the pastures on the hillsides a light film of snow had fallen, delicate as the veil of a bride adorned for the marriage; and as the childangel passed over them, alone in the swiftness of his flight, the pure fields sparkled round him, giving back his radiance.

And there were in that country shepherds abiding in the fields, keeping watch over their flocks by night. And lo! the angel of the Lord came upon them, and the glory of the Lord shone round about them, and they were sore afraid. And the angel   said unto them: "Fear not; for behold I bring you glad tidings of great joy which shall be to all nations. For unto you is born this day, in the city of David, a Saviour, which is Christ the Lord. And this shall be a sign unto you; ye shall find the babe wrapped in swaddling clothes, lying in a manger."

And suddenly there was with the angel a multitude of the heavenly host, praising God and saying: "Glory to God in the highest, and on earth peace, goodwill toward men." And the shepherds said one to another: "Let us now go, even to Bethlehem, and see this thing which is come to pass."

So I said within myself that I also would go with the shepherds, even to Bethlehem. And I heard a great and   sweet voice, as of a bell, which said, "Come!" And when the bell had sounded twelve times, I awoke; and it was Christmas morn; and I knew that I had been in a dream.

Yet it seemed to me that the things which I had heard were true.

A LITTLE ESSAY

CHRISTMASGIVING AND CHRISTMASLIVING

I

The custom of exchanging presents on a certain day in the year is very much older than Christmas, and means very much less. It has obtained in almost all ages of the world, and among many different nations. It is a fine thing or a foolish thing, as the case may be; an encouragement to friendliness, or a tribute to fashion; an expression of good nature, or a bid for favour; an outgoing of generosity, or a disguise of greed; a cheerful old custom, or a futile old farce, according to the   spirit which animates it and the form which it takes.

But when this ancient and variously interpreted tradition of a day of gifts was transferred to the Christmas season, it was brought into vital contact with an idea which must transform it, and with an example which must lift it up to a higher plane. The example is the life of Jesus. The idea is unselfish interest in the happiness of others.

The great gift of Jesus to the world was himself. He lived with and for men. He kept back nothing. In every particular and personal gift that he made to certain people there was something of himself that made it precious.

For example, at the wedding in Cana of Galilee, it was his thought   for the feelings of the giver of the feast, and his wish that every guest should find due entertainment, that lent the flavour of a heavenly hospitality to the wine which he provided.

When he gave bread and fish to the hungry multitude who had followed him out among the hills by the Lake of Gennesaret, the people were refreshed and strengthened by the sense of the personal care of Jesus for their welfare, as much as by the food which he bestowed upon them. It was another illustration of the sweetness of "a dinner of herbs, where love is."

The gifts of healing which he conferred upon many different kinds of sufferers were, in every case, evidences that Jesus was willing to give something of himself, his   thought, his sympathy, his vital power, to the men and women among whom he lived. Once, when a paralytic was brought to Jesus on a bed, he surprised everybody, and offended many, by giving the poor wretch the pardon of his sins, before he gave new life to his body. That was just because Jesus thought before he gave; because he desired to satisfy the deepest need; because in fact he gave something of himself in every gift. All true Christmasgiving ought to be after this pattern.

Not that it must all be solemn and serious. For the most part it deals with little wants, little joys, little tokens of friendly feeling. But the feeling must be more than the token; else the gift does not really belong to Christmas.

It takes time and effort and unselfish expenditure of strength to make gifts in this way. But it is the only way that fits the season.

The finest Christmas gift is not the one that costs the most money, but the one that carries the most love.

II

But how seldom Christmas comesonly once a year; and how soon it is overa night and a day! If that is the whole of it, it seems not much more durable than the little toys that one buys of a fakir on the streetcorner. They run for an hour, and then the spring breaks, and the legs come off, and nothing remains but a contribution to the dust heap.

But surely that need not and ought not to be the whole of Christmasonly   a single day of generosity, ransomed from the dull servitude of a selfish year,only a single night of merrymaking, celebrated in the slavequarters of a selfish race! If every gift is the token of a personal thought, a friendly feeling, an unselfish interest in the joy of others, then the thought, the feeling, the interest, may remain after the gift is made.

The little present, or the rare and longwishedfor gift (it matters not whether the vessel be of gold, or silver, or iron, or wood, or clay, or just a small bit of birch bark folded into a cup), may carry a message something like this:

"I am thinking of you today, because it is Christmas, and I wish you happiness. And tomorrow, because it   will be the day after Christmas, I shall still wish you happiness; and so on, clear through the year. I may not be able to tell you about it every day, because I may be far away; or because both of us may be very busy; or perhaps because I cannot even afford to pay the postage on so many letters, or find the time to write them. But that makes no difference. The thought and the wish will be here just the same. In my work and in the business of life, I mean to try not to be unfair to you or injure you in any way. In my pleasure, if we can be together, I would like to share the fun with you. Whatever joy or success comes to you will make me glad. Without pretense, and in plain words, goodwill to you is what I mean, in the Spirit of Christmas."

It is not necessary to put a message like this into highflown language, to swear absolute devotion and deathless consecration. In love and friendship, small, steady payments on a gold basis are better than immense promissory notes. Nor, indeed, is it always necessary to put the message into words at all, nor even to convey it by a tangible token. To feel it and to act it outthat is the main thing.

There are a great many people in the world whom we know more or less, but to whom for various reasons we cannot very well send a Christmas gift. But there is hardly one, in all the circles of our acquaintance, with whom we may not exchange the touch of Christmas life.

In the outer circles, cheerful greetings, courtesy, consideration; in the   inner circles, sympathetic interest, hearty congratulations, honest encouragement; in the inmost circle, comradeship, helpfulness, tenderness,

"Beautiful friendship tried by sun and wind
Durable from the daily dust of life."
After all, Christmasliving is the best kind of Christmasgiving.

A SHORT CHRISTMAS SERMON

KEEPING CHRISTMAS

ROMANS, He that regardeth the day, regardeth it unto the Lord.

It is a good thing to observe Christmas day. The mere marking of times and seasons, when men agree to stop work and make merry together, is a wise and wholesome custom. It helps one to feel the supremacy of the common life over the individual life. It reminds a man to set his own little watch, now and then, by the great clock of humanity which runs on sun time.

But there is a better thing than the observance of Christmas day, and that is, keeping Christmas.

Are you willing to forget what you have done for other people, and to remember what other people have done for you; to ignore what the world owes you, and to think what you owe the world; to put your rights in the background, and your duties in the middle distance, and your chances to do a little more than your duty in the foreground; to see that your fellowmen are just as real as you are, and try to look behind their faces to their hearts, hungry for joy; to own that probably the only good reason for your existence is not what you are going to get out of life, but what you are going to give to life; to close your book of complaints against the management of the universe, and look around you for a place where you can sow a few seeds   of happinessare you willing to do these things even for a day? Then you can keep Christmas.

Are you willing to stoop down and consider the needs and the desires of little children; to remember the weakness and loneliness of people who are growing old; to stop asking how much your friends love you, and ask yourself whether you love them enough; to bear in mind the things that other people have to bear on their hearts; to try to understand what those who live in the same house with you really want, without waiting for them to tell you; to trim your lamp so that it will give more light and less smoke, and to carry it in front so that your shadow will fall behind you; to make a grave for your ugly thoughts, and a garden for your kindly feelings, with the gate openare you willing to do these things even for a day? Then you can keep Christmas.

Are you willing to believe that love is the strongest thing in the worldstronger than hate, stronger than evil, stronger than deathand that the blessed life which began in Bethlehem nineteen hundred years ago is the image and brightness of the Eternal Love? Then you can keep Christmas.

And if you keep it for a day, why not always?

But you can never keep it alone.

TWO CHRISTMAS PRAYERS

A CHRISTMAS PRAYER FOR THE HOME

Father of all men, look upon our family,
Kneeling together before Thee,
And grant us a true Christmas.
With loving heart we bless Thee:
For the gift of Thy dear Son Jesus Christ,
For the peace He brings to human homes,
For the goodwill He teaches to sinful men,
For the glory of Thy goodness shining in His face.

With joyful voice we praise Thee:
For His lowly birth and His rest in the manger,
For the pure tenderness of His mother Mary,
For the fatherly care that protected Him,
For the Providence that saved the Holy Child
To be the Saviour of the world.
With deep desire we beseech Thee:
Help us to keep His birthday truly,
Help us to offer, in His name, our Christmas prayer.
From the sickness of sin and the darkness of doubt,
From selfish pleasures and sullen pains,

From the frost of pride and the fever of envy,
God save us every one, through the blessing of Jesus.
In the health of purity and the calm of mutual trust,
In the sharing of joy and the bearing of trouble,
In the steady glow of love and the clear light of hope,
God keep us every one, by the blessing of Jesus.
In praying and praising, in giving and receiving,
In eating and drinking, in singing and making merry,
In parents' gladness and in children's mirth,
In dear memories of those who have departed,

In good comradeship with those who are here,
In kind wishes for those who are far away,
In patient waiting, sweet contentment, generous cheer,
God bless us every one, with the blessing of Jesus.
By remembering our kinship with all men,

By wellwishing, friendly speaking and kindly doing,
By cheering the downcast and adding sunshine to daylight,
By welcoming strangers (poor shepherds or wise men),
By keeping the music of the angels' song in this home,
God help us every one to share the blessing of Jesus:

In whose name we keep Christmas:
And in whose words we pray together:
Our Father which art in heaven, hallowed be Thy name.
Thy kingdom come. Thy will be done in earth, as it is in heaven.
Give us this day our daily bread. And forgive us our debts, as we forgive our debtors.
And lead us not into temptation, but deliver us from evil:
For Thine is the kingdom, and the power, and the glory, forever. Amen.

A CHRISTMAS PRAYER FOR LONELY FOLKS

Lord God of the solitary,
Look upon me in my loneliness.
Since I may not keep this Christmas in the home,
Send it into my heart.
Let not my sins cloud me in,
But shine through them with forgiveness in the face of the child Jesus.
Put me in loving remembrance of the lowly lodging in the stable of Bethlehem,
The sorrows of the blessed Mary, the poverty and exile of the Prince of Peace.

For His sake, give me a cheerful courage to endure my lot,
And an inward comfort to sweeten it.
Purge my heart from hard and bitter thoughts.
Let no shadow of forgetting come between me and friends far away:
Bless them in their Christmas mirth:
Hedge me in with faithfulness,
That I may not grow unworthy to meet them again.
Give me good work to do,
That I may forget myself and find peace in doing it for Thee.
Though I am poor, send me to carry some gift to those who are poorer,

Some cheer to those who are more lonely.
Grant me the joy to do a kindness to one of Thy little ones:
Light my Christmas candle at the gladness of an innocent and grateful heart.
Strange is the path where Thou leadest me:
Let me not doubt Thy wisdom, nor lose Thy hand.
Make me sure that Eternal Love is revealed in Jesus, Thy dear Son,
To save us from sin and solitude and death.
Teach me that I am not alone,
But that many hearts, all round the world,
Join with me through the silence, while I pray in His name:

Our Father which art in heaven, hallowed be Thy name.
Thy kingdom come. Thy will be done in earth, as it is in heaven.
Give us this day our daily bread. And forgive us our debts, as we forgive our debtors.
And lead us not into temptation, but deliver us from evil:
For Thine is the kingdom, and the power, and the glory, forever. Amen.

The Keeper Of The Light

By

Henry Van Dyke

THE KEEPER OF THE LIGHT

At long distance, looking over the blue waters of the Gulf of St. Lawrence in clear weather, you might think that you saw a lonely seagull, snowwhite, perching motionless on a cobble of gray rock. Then, as your boat drifted in, following the languid tide and the soft southern breeze, you would perceive that the cobble of rock was a rugged hill with a few bushes and stunted trees growing in the crevices, and that the gleaming speck near the summit must be some kind of a buildingif you were on the coast of Italy or Spain you would say a villa or a farmhouse. Then, as you floated still farther north and drew nearer to the coast, the desolate hill would detach itself from the mainland and become a little mountainisle, with a flock of smaller islets clustering around it as a brood of wild ducks keep close to their mother, and with deep water, nearly two miles wide, flowing between it and the shore; while the shining speck on the seaward side stood out clearly as a low, whitewashed dwelling with a sturdy round tower at one end, crowned with a big eightsided lanterna solitary lighthouse.

That is the Isle of the Wise Virgin. Behind it the long blue Laurentian Mountains, clothed with unbroken forest, rise in sombre ranges toward the Height of Land. In front of it the waters of the gulf heave and sparkle far away to where the dim peaks of St. Anne des Monts are traced along the southern horizon. Sheltered a little, but not completely, by the island breakwater of granite, lies the rocky beach of Dead Men's Point, where an English navy was wrecked in a night of storm a hundred years ago.

There are a score of wooden houses, a tiny, weatherbeaten chapel, a Hudson Bay Company's store, a row of platforms for drying fish, and a varied assortment of boats and nets, strung along the beach now. Dead Men's Point has developed into a centre of industry, with a life, a tradition, a social character of its own. And in one of those houses, as you sit at the door in the lingering June twilight, looking out across the deep channel to where the lantern of the tower is just beginning to glow with orange radiance above the shadow of the islandin that faraway place, in that mystical hour, you should hear the story of the light and its keeper.

When the lighthouse was built, many years ago, the island had another name. It was called the Isle of Birds. Thousands of seafowl nested there. The handful of people who lived on the shore robbed the nests and slaughtered the birds, with considerable profit. It was perceived in advance that the building of the lighthouse would interfere with this, and with other things. Hence it was not altogether a popular improvement. Marcel Thibault, the oldest inhabitant, was the leader of the opposition.

"That lighthouse!" said he, "what good will it be for us? We know the way in and out when it makes clear weather, by day or by night. But when the sky gets swampy, when it makes fog, then we stay with ourselves at home, or we run into La Trinite, or Pentecote. We know the way. What? The stranger boats? B'EN! the stranger boats need not to come here, if they know not the way. The more fish, the more seals, the more everything will there be left for us. Just because of the stranger boats, to build something that makes all the birds wild and spoils the huntingthat is a fool's work. The good God made no stupid light on the Isle of Birds. He saw no necessity of it."

"Besides," continued Thibault, puffing slowly at his pipe, "besidesthose stranger boats, sometimes they are lost, they come ashore. It is sad! But who gets the things that are saved, all sorts of things, good to put into our houses, good to eat, good to sell, sometimes a boat that can be patched up almost like newwho gets these things, eh? Doubtless those for whom the good God intended them. But who shall get them when this sacre lighthouse is built, eh? Tell me that, you Baptiste Fortin."

Fortin represented the party of progress in the little parliament of the beach. He had come down from Quebec some years ago bringing with him a wife and two little daughters, and a good many new notions about life. He had good luck at the codfishing, and built a house with windows at the side as well as in front. When his third girl, Nataline, was born, he went so far as to paint the house red, and put on a kitchen, and enclose a bit of ground for a yard. This marked him as a radical, an innovator. It was expected that he would defend the building of the lighthouse. And he did.

"Monsieur Thibault," he said, "you talk well, but you talk too late. It is of a past age, your talk. A new time comes to the Cote Nord. We begin to civilize ourselves. To hold back against the light would be our shame. Tell me this, Marcel Thibault, what men are they that love darkness?"

"TORRIEUX!" growled Thibault, "that is a little strong. You say my deeds are evil?"

"No, no," answered Fortin; "I say not that, my friend, but I say this lighthouse means good: good for us, and good for all who come to this coast. It will bring more trade to us. It will bring a boat with the mail, with newspapers, perhaps once, perhaps twice a month, all through the summer. It will bring us into the great world. To lose that for the sake of a few birdsCA SERA B'EN DE VALEUR! Besides, it is impossible. The lighthouse is coming, certain."

Fortin was right, of course. But Thibault's position was not altogether unnatural, nor unfamiliar. All over the world, for the past hundred years, people have been kicking against the sharpness of the pricks that drove them forward out of the old life, the wild life, the free life, grown dear to them because it was so easy. There has been a terrible interference with birdnesting and other things. All over the world the great Something that bridges rivers, and tunnels mountains, and fells forests, and populates deserts, and opens up the hidden corners of the earth, has been pushing steadily on; and the people who like things to remain as they are have had to give up a great deal. There was no exception made in favour of Dead Men's Point. The Isle of Birds lay in the line of progress. The lighthouse arrived.

It was a very good house for that day. The keeper's dwelling had three rooms and was solidly built. The tower was thirty feet high. The lantern held a revolving light, with a fourwick Fresnel lamp, burning sperm oil. There was one of Stevenson's new cages of dioptric prisms around the flame, and once every minute it was turned by clockwork, flashing a broad belt of radiance fifteen miles across the sea. All night long that big bright eye was opening and shutting. "BAGUETTE!" said Thibault, "it winks like a oneeyed Windigo."

The Department of Marine and Fisheries sent down an expert from Quebec to keep the light in order and run it for the first summer. He took Fortin as his assistant. By the end of August he reported to headquarters that the light was all right, and that Fortin was qualified to be appointed keeper. Before October was out the certificate of appointment came back, and the expert packed his bag to go up the river.

"Now look here, Fortin," said he, "this is no fishing trip. Do you think you are up to this job?"

"I suppose," said Fortin.

"Well now, do you remember all this business about the machinery that turns the lenses? That 's the main thing. The bearings must be kept well oiled, and the weight must never get out of order. The clockface will tell you when it is running right. If anything gets hitched up here's the crank to keep it going until you can straighten the machine again. It's easy enough to turn it. But you must never let it stop between dark and daylight. The regular turn once a minutethat's the mark of this light. If it shines steady it might as well be out. Yes, better! Any vessel coming along here in a dirty night and seeing a fixed light would take it for the Cap LoupMarin and run ashore. This particular light has got to revolve once a minute every night from April first to December tenth, certain. Can you do it?"

"Certain," said Fortin.

"That's the way I like to hear a man talk! Now, you've got oil enough to last you through till the tenth of December, when you close the light, and to run on for a month in the spring after you open again. The ice may be late in going out and perhaps the supplyboat can't get down before the middle of April, or thereabouts. But she'll bring plenty of oil when she comes, so you'll be all right."

"All right," said Fortin.

"Well, I've said it all, I guess. You understand what you've got to do? Goodby and good luck. You're the keeper of the light now."

"Good luck," said Fortin, "I am going to keep it." The same day he shut up the red house on the beach and moved to the white house on the island with MarieAnne, his wife, and the three girls, Alma, aged seventeen, Azilda, aged fifteen, and Nataline, aged thirteen. He was the captain, and MarieAnne was the mate, and the three girls were the crew. They were all as full of happy pride as if they had come into possession of a great fortune.

It was the thirtyfirst day of October. A snowshower had silvered the island. The afternoon was clear and beautiful. As the sun sloped toward the rosecoloured hills of the mainland the whole family stood out in front of the lighthouse looking up at the tower.

"Regard him well, my children," said Baptiste; "God has given him to us to keep, and to keep us. Thibault says he is a Windigo. B'EN! We shall see that he is a friendly Windigo. Every minute all the night he shall wink, just for kindness and good luck to all the world, till the daylight."

II

On the ninth of November, at three o'clock in the afternoon, Baptiste went into the tower to see that the clockwork was in order for the night. He set the dial on the machine, put a few drops of oil on the bearings of the cylinder, and started to wind up the weight.

It rose a few inches, gave a dull click, and then stopped dead. He tugged a little harder, but it would not move. Then he tried to let it down. He pushed at the lever that set the clockwork in motion.

He might as well have tried to make the island turn around by pushing at one of the little spruce trees that clung to the rock.

Then it dawned fearfully upon him that something must be wrong. Trembling with anxiety, he climbed up and peered in among the wheels.

The escapement wheel was cracked clean through, as if some one had struck it with the head of an axe, and one of the pallets of the spindle was stuck fast in the crack. He could knock it out easily enough, but when the crack came around again, the pallet would catch and the clock would stop once more. It was a fatal injury.

Baptiste turned white, then red, gripped his head in his hands, and ran down the steps, out of the door, straight toward his canoe, which was pulled up on the western side of the island.

"DAME!" he cried, "who has done this? Let me catch him! If that old Thibault"

As he leaped down the rocky slope the setting sun gleamed straight in his eyes. It was poised like a ball of fire on the very edge of the mountains. Five minutes more and it would be gone. Fifteen minutes more and darkness would close in. Then the giant's eye must begin to glow, and to wink precisely once a minute all night long. If not, what became of the keeper's word, his faith, his honour?

No matter how the injury to the clockwork was done. No matter who was to be blamed or punished for it. That could wait. The question now was whether the light would fail or not. And it must be answered within a quarter of an hour.

That red ray of the vanishing sun was like a blow in the face to Baptiste. It stopped him short, dazed and bewildered. Then he came to himself, wheeled, and ran up the rocks faster than he had come down.

"MarieAnne! Alma!" he shouted, as he dashed past the door of the house, "all of you! To me, in the tower!"

He was up in the lantern when they came running in, full of curiosity, excited, asking twenty questions at once. Nataline climbed up the ladder and put her head through the trapdoor.

"What is it?" she panted. "What has hap"

"Go down," answered her father, "go down all at once. Wait for me. I am coming. I will explain."

The explanation was not altogether lucid and scientific. There were some bad words mixed up with it.

Baptiste was still hot with anger and the unsatisfied desire to whip somebody, he did not know whom, for something, he did not know what. But angry as he was, he was still sane enough to hold his mind hard and close to the main point. The crank must be adjusted; the machine must be ready to turn before dark. While he worked he hastily made the situation clear to his listeners.

That crank must be turned by hand, round and round all night, not too slow, not too fast. The dial on the machine must mark time with the clock on the wall. The light must flash once every minute until daybreak. He would do as much of the labour as he could, but the wife and the two older girls must help him. Nataline could go to bed.

At this Nataline's short upper lip trembled. She rubbed her eyes with the sleeve of her dress, and began to weep silently.

"What is the matter with you?" said her mother, "bad child, have you fear to sleep alone? A big girl like you!"

"No," she sobbed, "I have no fear, but I want some of the fun."

"Fun!" growled her father. "What fun? NOM D'UN CHIEN! She calls this fun!" He looked at her for a moment, as she stood there, half defiant, half despondent, with her red mouth quivering and her big brown eyes sparkling fire; then he burst into a hearty laugh.

"Come here, my little wildcat," he said, drawing her to him and kissing her; "you are a good girl after all. I suppose you think this light is part yours, eh?"

The girl nodded.

"B'EN! You shall have your share, fun and all. You shall make the tea for us and bring us something to eat. Perhaps when Alma and 'Zilda fatigue themselves they will permit a few turns of the crank to you. Are you content? Run now and boil the kettle."

It was a very long night. No matter how easily a handle turns, after a certain number of revolutions there is a stiffness about it. The stiffness is not in the handle, but in the hand that pushes it.

Round and round, evenly, steadily, minute after minute, hour after hour, shoving out, drawing in, circle after circle, no swerving, no stopping, no varying the motion, turn after turnfiftyfive, fiftysix, fiftysevenwhat's the use of counting? Watch the dial; go to sleepno! for God's sake, no sleep! But how hard it is to keep awake! How heavy the arm grows, how stiffly the muscles move, how the will creaks and groans. BATISCAN! It is not easy for a human being to become part of a machine.

Fortin himself took the longest spell at the crank, of course. He went at his work with a rigid courage. His redhot anger had cooled down into a shape that was like a bar of forged steel. He meant to make that light revolve if it killed him to do it. He was the captain of a company that had run into an ambuscade. He was going to fight his way through if he had to fight alone.

The wife and the two older girls followed him blindly and bravely, in the habit of sheer obedience. They did not quite understand the meaning of the task, the honour of victory, the shame of defeat. But Fortin said it must be done, and he knew best. So they took their places in turn, as he grew weary, and kept the light flashing.

And Natalinewell, there is no way of describing what Nataline did, except to say that she played the fife.

She felt the contest just as her father did, not as deeply, perhaps, but in the same spirit. She went into the fight with darkness like a little soldier. And she played the fife.

When she came up from the kitchen with the smoking pail of tea, she rapped on the door and called out to know whether the Windigo was at home tonight.

She ran in and out of the place like a squirrel. She looked up at the light and laughed. Then she ran in and reported. "He winks," she said, "old oneeye winks beautifully. Keep him going. My turn now!"

She refused to be put off with a shorter spell than the other girls. "No," she cried, "I can do it as well as you. You think you are so much older. Well, what of that? The light is part mine; father said so. Let me turn, vaten."

When the first glimmer of the little day came shivering along the eastern horizon, Nataline was at the crank. The mother and the two older girls were half asleep. Baptiste stepped out to look at the sky. "Come," he cried, returning. "We can stop now, it is growing gray in the east, almost morning."

"But not yet," said Nataline; "we must wait for the first red. A few more turns. Let's finish it up with a song."

She shook her head and piped up the refrain of the old Canadian chanson:

"En roulant ma boulele roulant

En roulant ma boule."

And to that cheerful music the first night's battle was carried through to victory.

The next day Fortin spent two hours in trying to repair the clockwork. It was of no use. The broken part was indispensable and could not be replaced.

At noon he went over to the mainland to tell of the disaster, and perhaps to find out if any hostile hand was responsible for it. He found out nothing. Every one denied all knowledge of the accident. Perhaps there was a flaw in the wheel; perhaps it had broken itself. That was possible. Fortin could not deny it; but the thing that hurt him most was that he got so little sympathy. Nobody seemed to care whether the light was kept burning or not. When he told them how the machine had been turned all night by hand, they were astonished. "CREIE!" they cried, "you must have had a great misery to do that." But that he proposed to go on doing it for a month longer, until December tenth, and to begin again on April first, and go on turning the light by hand for three or four weeks more until the supplyboat came down and brought the necessary tools to repair the machinesuch an idea as this went beyond their horizon.

"But you are crazy, Baptiste," they said, "you can never do it; you are not capable."

"I would be crazy," he answered, "if I did not see what I must do. That light is my charge. In all the world there is nothing else so great as that for me and for my familyyou understand? For us it is the chief thing. It is my Ten Commandments. I shall keep it or be damned."

There was a silence after this remark. They were not very particular about the use of language at Dead Men's Point, but this shocked them a little. They thought that Fortin was swearing a shade too hard. In reality he was never more reverent, never more soberly in earnest.

After a while he continued, "I want some one to help me with the work on the island. We must be up all the nights now. By day we must get some sleep. I want another man or a strong boy. Is there any who will come? The Government will pay. Or if not, I will pay, moimeme."

There was no response. All the men hung back. The lighthouse was still unpopular, or at least it was on trial. Fortin's pluck and resolution had undoubtedly impressed them a little. But they still hesitated to commit themselves to his side.

"B'en," he said, "there is no one. Then we shall manage the affair en famille. Bon soir, messieurs!"

He walked down to the beach with his head in the air, without looking back. But before he had his canoe in the water he heard some one running down behind him. It was Thibault's youngest son, Marcel, a wellgrown boy of sixteen, very much out of breath with running and shyness.

"Monsieur Fortin," he stammered, "will youdo you thinkam I big enough?"

Baptiste looked him in the face for a moment. Then his eyes twinkled.

"Certain," he answered, "you are bigger than your father. But what will he say to this?"

"He says," blurted out Marcel"well, he says that he will say nothing if I do not ask him."

So the little Marcel was enlisted in the crew on the island. For thirty nights those six peoplea man, and a boy, and four women (Nataline was not going to submit to any distinctions on the score of age, you may be sure)for a full month they turned their flashing lantern by hand from dusk to daybreak.

The fog, the frost, the hail, the snow beleaguered their tower. Hunger and cold, sleeplessness and weariness, pain and discouragement, held rendezvous in that dismal, cramped little room. Many a night Nataline's fife of fun played a feeble, wheezy note. But it played. And the crank went round. And every bit of glass in the lantern was as clear as polished crystal. And the big lamp was full of oil. And the great eye of the friendly giant winked without ceasing, through fierce storm and placid moonlight.

When the tenth of December came, the light went to sleep for the winter, and the keepers took their way across the ice to the mainland. They had won the battle, not only on the island, fighting against the elements, but also at Dead Men's Point, against public opinion. The inhabitants began to understand that the lighthouse meant somethinga law, an order, a principle.

Men cannot help feeling respect for a thing when they see others willing to fight or to suffer for it.

When the time arrived to kindle the light again in the spring, Fortin could have had any one that he wanted to help him. But no; he chose the little Marcel again; the boy wanted to go, and he had earned the right. Besides, he and Nataline had struck up a close friendship on the island, cemented during the winter by various hunting excursions after hares and ptarmigan. Marcel was a skilful setter of snares. But Nataline was not content until she had won consent to borrow her father's CARABINE. They hunted in partnership. One day they had shot a fox. That is, Nataline had shot it, though Marcel had seen it first and tracked it. Now they wanted to try for a seal on the point of the island when the ice went out. It was quite essential that Marcel should go.

"Besides," said Baptiste to his wife, confidentially, "a boy costs less than a man. Why should we waste money? Marcel is best."

A peasanthero is seldom averse to economy in small things, like money.

But there was not much play in the spring session with the light on the island. It was a bitter job. December had been lamblike compared with April. First, the southeast wind kept the ice driving in along the shore. Then the northwest wind came hurtling down from the Arctic wilderness like a pack of wolves. There was a snowstorm of four days and nights that made the whole worldearth and sky and sealook like a crazy white chaos. And through it all, that weary, dogged crank must be kept turningturning from dark to daylight.

It seemed as if the supplyboat would never come. At last they saw it, one fair afternoon, April the twentyninth, creeping slowly down the coast. They were just getting ready for another night's work.

Fortin ran out of the tower, took off his hat, and began to say his prayers. The wife and the two elder girls stood in the kitchen door, crossing themselves, with tears in their eyes. Marcel and Nataline were coming up from the point of the island, where they had been watching for their seal. She was singing

"Mon pere n'avait fille que moi,

Encore sur la mer il m'envoieeh!"

When she saw the boat she stopped short for a minute.

"Well," she said, "they find us awake, n'estc'pas? And if they don't come faster than that we'll have another chance to show them how we make the light wink, eh?"

Then she went on with her song

"Sautez, mignonne, Cecilia.

Ah, ah, ah, ah, Cecilia!"

III

You did not suppose that was the end of the story, did you?

No, an outofdoors story does not end like that, broken off in the middle, with a bit of a song. It goes on to something definite, like a wedding or a funeral.

You have not heard, yet, how near the light came to failing, and how the keeper saved it and something else too. Nataline's story is not told; it is only begun. This first part is only the introduction, just to let you see what kind of a girl she was, and how her life was made. If you want to hear the conclusion, we must hurry along a little faster or we shall never get to it.

Nataline grew up like a young birch treestately and strong, good to look at. She was beautiful in her place; she fitted it exactly. Her bronzed face with an undertinge of red; her low, black eyebrows; her clear eyes like the brown waters of a woodland stream; her dark, curly hair with little tendrils always blowing loose around the pillar of her neck; her broad breast and sloping shoulders; her firm, fearless step; her voice, rich and vibrant; her straight, steady looksbut there, who can describe a thing like that? I tell you she was a girl to love outofdoors.

There was nothing that she could not do. She could cook; she could swing an axe; she could paddle a canoe; she could fish; she could shoot; and, best of all, she could run the lighthouse. Her father's devotion to it had gone into her blood. It was the centre of her life, her law of God. There was nothing about it that she did not understand and love. From the first of April to the tenth of December the flashing of that light was like the beating of her heartsteady, even, unfaltering. She kept time to it as unconsciously as the tides follow the moon. She lived by it and for it.

There were no more accidents to the clockwork after the first one was repaired. It ran on regularly, year after year.

Alma and Azilda were married and went away to live, one on the South Shore, the other at Quebec. Nataline was her father's righthand man. As the rheumatism took hold of him and lamed his shoulders and wrists, more and more of the work fell upon her. She was proud of it.

At last it came to pass, one day in January, that Baptiste died. He was not gathered to his fathers, for they were buried far away beside the Montmorenci, and on the rocky coast of Brittany. But the men dug through the snow behind the tiny chapel at Dead Men's Point, and made a grave for Baptiste Fortin, and the young priest of the mission read the funeral service over it.

It went without saying that Nataline was to be the keeper of the light, at least until the supplyboat came down again in the spring and orders arrived from the Government in Quebec. Why not? She was a woman, it is true. But if a woman can do a thing as well as a man, why should she not do it? Besides, Nataline could do this particular thing much better than any man on the Point. Everybody approved of her as the heir of her father, especially young Marcel Thibault.

What?

Yes, of course. You could not help guessing it. He was Nataline's lover. They were to be married the next summer. They sat together in the best room, while the old mother was rocking to and fro and knitting beside the kitchen stove, and talked of what they were going to do. Once in a while, when Nataline grieved for her father, she would let Marcel put his arm around her and comfort her in the way that lovers know. But their talk was mainly of the future, because they were young, and of the light, because Nataline's life belonged to it.

Perhaps the Government would remember that year when it was kept going by hand for two months, and give it to her to keep as long as she lived. That would be only fair. Certainly, it was hers for the present. No one had as good a right to it. She took possession without a doubt. At all events, while she was the keeper the light should not fail.

But that winter was a bad one on the North Shore, and particularly at Dead Men's Point. It was terribly bad. The summer before, the fishing had been almost a dead failure. In June a wild storm had smashed all the salmon nets and swept most of them away. In July they could find no caplin for bait for the codfishing, and in August and September they could find no cod. The few bushels of potatoes that some of the inhabitants had planted, rotted in the ground. The people at the Point went into the winter short of money and very short of food.

There were some supplies at the store, pork and flour and molasses, and they could run through the year on credit and pay their debts the following summer if the fish came back. But this resource also failed them. In the last week of January the store caught fire and burned up. Nothing was saved. The only hope now was the sealhunting in February and March and April. That at least would bring them meat and oil enough to keep them from starvation.

But this hope failed, too. The winds blew strong from the north and west, driving the ice far out into the gulf. The chase was long and perilous. The seals were few and wild. Less than a dozen were killed in all. By the last week in March Dead Men's Point stood face to face with famine.

Then it was that old Thibault had an idea.

"There is sperm oil on the Island of Birds," said he, "in the lighthouse, plenty of it, gallons of it. It is not very good to taste, perhaps, but what of that? It will keep life in the body. The Esquimaux drink it in the north, often. We must take the oil of the lighthouse to keep us from starving until the supplyboat comes down."

"But how shall we get it?" asked the others. "It is locked up. Nataline Fortin has the key. Will she give it?"

"Give it?" growled Thibault. "Name of a name! of course she will give it. She must. Is not a life, the life of all of us, more than a light?"

A selfappointed committee of three, with Thibault at the head, waited upon Nataline without delay, told her their plan, and asked for the key. She thought it over silently for a few minutes, and then refused pointblank.

"No," she said, "I will not give the key. That oil is for the lamp. If you take it, the lamp will not be lighted on the first of April; it will not be burning when the supplyboat comes. For me, that would be shame, disgrace, worse than death. I am the keeper of the light. You shall not have the oil."

They argued with her, pleaded with her, tried to browbeat her. She was a rock. Her round underjaw was set like a steel trap. Her lips straightened into a white line. Her eyebrows drew together, and her eyes grew black.

"No," she cried, "I tell you no, no, a thousand times no. All in this house I will share with you. But not one drop of what belongs to the light! Never."

Later in the afternoon the priest came to see her; a thin, pale young man, bent with the hardships of his life, and with sad dreams in his sunken eyes. He talked with her very gently and kindly.

"Think well, my daughter; think seriously what you do. Is it not our first duty to save human life? Surely that must be according to the will of God. Will you refuse to obey it?"

Nataline was trembling a little now. Her brows were unlocked. The tears stood in her eyes and ran down her cheeks. She was twisting her hands together.

"My father," she answered, "I desire to do the will of God. But how shall I know it? Is it not His first command that we should love and serve Him faithfully in the duty which He has given us? He gave me this light to keep. My father kept it. He is dead. If I am unfaithful what will he say to me? Besides, the supplyboat is coming soonI have thought of thiswhen it comes it will bring food. But if the light is out, the boat may be lost. That would be the punishment for my sin. No, MON PERE, we must trust God. He will keep the people. I will keep the light."'

The priest looked at her long and steadily. A glow came into his face. He put his hand on her shoulder. "You shall follow your conscience," he said quietly. "Peace be with you, Nataline."

That evening just at dark Marcel came. She let him take her in his arms and kiss her. She felt like a little child, tired and weak.

"Well," he whispered, "you have done bravely, sweetheart. You were right not to give the key. That would have been a shame to you. But it is all settled now. They will have the oil without your fault. Tonight they are going out to the lighthouse to break in and take what they want. You need not know. There will be no blame"

She straightened in his arms as if an electric shock had passed through her. She sprang back, blazing with anger.

"What?" she cried, "me a thief by roundabout,with my hand behind my back and my eyes shut? Never. Do you think I care only for the blame? I tell you that is nothing. My light shall not be robbed, never, never!"

She came close to him and took him by the shoulders. Their eyes were on a level. He was a strong man, but she was the stronger then.

"Marcel Thibault," she said, "do you love me?"

"My faith," he gasped, "I do. You know I do."

"Then listen," she continued; "this is what you are going to do. You are going down to the shore at once to make ready the big canoe. I am going to get food enough to last us for the month. It will be a hard pinch, but it will do. Then we are going out to the island tonight, in less than an hour. Day after tomorrow is the first of April. Then we shall light the lantern, and it shall burn every night until the boat comes down. You hear? Now go: and be quick and bring your gun."

IV

They pushed off in the black darkness, among the fragments of ice that lay along the shore. They crossed the strait in silence, and hid their canoe among the rocks on the island. They carried their stuff up to the house and locked it in the kitchen. Then they unlocked the tower, and went in, Marcel with his shotgun, and Nataline with her father's old carabine. They fastened the door again, and bolted it, and sat down in the dark to wait.

Presently they heard the grating of the prow of the barge on the stones below, the steps of men stumbling up the steep path, and voices mingled in confused talk. The glimmer of a couple of lanterns went bobbing in and out among the rocks and bushes. There was a little crowd of eight or ten men, and they came on carelessly, chattering and laughing. Three of them carried axes, and three others a heavy log of wood which they had picked up on their way.

"The log is better than the axes," said one; "take it in your hands this way, two of you on one side, another on the opposite side in the middle. Then swing it back and forwards and let it go. The door will come down, I tell you, like a sheet of paper. But wait till I give the word, then swing hard. Onetwo"

"Stop!" cried Nataline, throwing open the little window. "If you dare to touch that door, I shoot."

She thrust out the barrel of the rifle, and Marcel's shotgun appeared beside it. The old rifle was not loaded, but who knew that? Besides, both barrels of the shotgun were full.

There was amazement in the crowd outside the tower, and consternation, and then anger.

"Marcel," they shouted, "you there? MAUDIT POLISSON! Come out of that. Let us in. You told us"

"I know," answered Marcel, "but I was mistaken, that is all. I stand by Mademoiselle Fortin. What she says is right. If any man tries to break in here, we kill him. No more talk!"

The gang muttered; cursed; threatened; looked at the guns; and went off to their boat.

"It is murder that you will do," one of them called out, "you are a murderess, you Mademoiselle Fortin! you cause the people to die of hunger!"

"Not I," she answered; "that is as the good God pleases. No matter. The light shall burn."

They heard the babble of the men as they stumbled down the hill; the grinding of the boat on the rocks as they shoved off; the rattle of the oars in the rowlocks. After that the island was as still as a graveyard.

Then Nataline sat down on the floor in the dark, and put her face in her hands, and cried. Marcel tried to comfort her. She took his hand and pushed it gently away from her waist.

"No, Marcel," she said, "not now! Not that, please, Marcel! Come into the house. I want to talk with you."

They went into the cold, dark kitchen, lit a candle and kindled a fire in the stove. Nataline busied herself with a score of things. She put away the poor little store of provisions, sent Marcel for a pail of water, made some tea, spread the table, and sat down opposite to him. For a time she kept her eyes turned away from him, while she talked about all sorts of things. Then she fell silent for a little, still not looking at him. She got up and moved about the room, arranged two or three packages on the shelves, shut the damper of the stove, glancing at Marcel's back out of the corners of her eyes. Then she came back to her chair, pushed her cup aside, rested both elbows on the table and her chin in her hands, and looked Marcel square in the face with her clear brown eyes.

"My friend," she said, "are you an honest man, un brave garcon?"

For an instant he could say nothing. He was so puzzled. "Why yes, Nataline," he answered, "yes, surelyI hope."

"Then let me speak to you without fear," she continued. "You do not suppose that I am ignorant of what I have done this night. I am not a baby. You are a man. I am a girl. We are shut up alone in this house for two weeks, a month, God knows how long. You know what that means, what people will say. I have risked all that a girl has most precious. I have put my good name in your hands."

Marcel tried to speak, but she stopped him.

"Let me finish. It is not easy to say. I know you are honourable. I trust you waking and sleeping. But I am a woman. There must be no lovemaking. We have other work to do. The light must not fail. You will not touch me, you will not embrace menot oncetill after the boat has come. Then"she smiled at him like a sunburned angel"well, is it a bargain?"

She put out one hand across the table. Marcel took it in both of his own. He did not kiss it. He lifted it up in front of his face.

"I swear to you, Nataline, you shall be to me as the Blessed Virgin herself."

The next day they put the light in order, and the following night they kindled it. They still feared another attack from the mainland, and thought it needful that one of them should be on guard all the time, though the machine itself was working beautifully and needed little watching. Nataline took the night duty; it was her own choice; she loved the charge of the lamp. Marcel was on duty through the day. They were together for three or four hours in the morning and in the evening.

It was not a desperate vigil like that affair with the broken clockwork eight years before. There was no weary turning of the crank. There was just enough work to do about the house and the tower to keep them busy. The weather was fair. The worst thing was the short supply of food. But though they were hungry, they were not starving. And Nataline still played the fife. She jested, she sang, she told long fairy stories while they sat in the kitchen. Marcel admitted that it was not at all a bad arrangement.

But his thoughts turned very often to the arrival of the supplyboat. He hoped it would not be late. The ice was well broken up already and driven far out into the gulf. The boat ought to be able to run down the shore in good time.

One evening as Nataline came down from her sleep she saw Marcel coming up the rocks dragging a young seal behind him.

"Hurra!" he shouted, "here is plenty of meat. I shot it out at the end of the island, about an hour ago."

But Nataline said that they did not need the seal. There was still food enough in the larder. On shore there must be greater need. Marcel must take the seal over to the mainland that night and leave it on the beach near the priest's house. He grumbled a little, but he did it.

That was on the twentythird of April. The clear sky held for three days longer, calm, bright, halcyon weather. On the afternoon of the twentyseventh the clouds came down from the north, not a long furious tempest, but a brief, sharp storm, with considerable wind and a whirling, blinding fall of April snow. It was a bad night for boats at sea, confusing, bewildering, a night when the lighthouse had to do its best. Nataline was in the tower all night, tending the lamp, watching the clockwork. Once it seemed to her that the lantern was so covered with snow that light could not shine through. She got her long brush and scraped the snow away. It was cold work, but she gloried in it. The bright eye of the tower, winking, winking steadily through the storm seemed to be the sign of her power in the world. It was hers. She kept it shining.

When morning came the wind was still blowing fitfully off shore, but the snow had almost ceased. Nataline stopped the clockwork, and was just climbing up into the lantern to put out the lamp, when Marcel's voice hailed her.

"Come down, Nataline, come down quick. Make haste!"

She turned and hurried out, not knowing what was to come; perhaps a message of trouble from the mainland, perhaps a new assault on the lighthouse.

As she came out of the tower, her brown eyes heavy from the nightwatch, her dark face pale from the cold, she saw Marcel standing on the rocky knoll beside the house and pointing shoreward.

She ran up beside him and looked. There, in the deep water between the island and the point, lay the supplyboat, rocking quietly on the waves.

It flashed upon her in a moment what it meantthe end of her fight, relief for the village, victory! And the light that had guided the little ship safe through the stormy night into the harbour was hers.

She turned and looked up at the lamp, still burning.

"I kept you!" she cried.

Then she turned to Marcel; the colour rose quickly in her cheeks, the light sparkled in her eyes; she smiled, and held out both her hands, whispering, "Now you shall keep me!"

There was a fine wedding on the last day of April, and from that time the island took its new name,the Isle of the Wise Virgin.